MILEY'S M...

 # Katie Goodacre

First published in Great Britain 2020
by Pink Parties Press
Copperhill
1 Ermine Street
Ancaster
Lincolnshire NG32 3PL

Acknowledgements

Natasha Aspden
for her help with the book title
Edward and William B, Lily J, Sky and Halle B, Emma C and Ben H
for their help to select the front cover
Dr Heather Goodacre and Dr Michael McArdle
for their advice on wording.

Dedication

To Dr Katy Bloom
Thank you, for all that you have done.

To Lily J, Sky B and all the wonderful children
I had the pleasure of working with, in 2017-2018,
at St. Nicholas Church of England Primary School,
Blackpool, Lancashire.

"When we can talk about our feelings, they become less overwhelming, less upsetting, and less scary. The people we trust with that important talk can help us know that we are not alone."

Fred Rogers

Miley was a happy dog... or so everyone thought.

Each morning, she would...

...sing to the sun and dance among the dew.

When it rained, she would...

...clap the clouds for

helping the flowers to bloom

and burble all about

her day to the moon.

People used to say, "Gosh Miley, how smiley you are!"

But Miley had a secret. A secret she was scared to share...

...Miley had a poorly mind. Like a broken leg and a sickly tummy,

Miley's mind needed a bit of looking after.

You see, people were not always kind to Miley.

Not everyone treated Miley with respect...

...and Miley had lost people she loved.

All of these things had made
her feel sad and caused her mind
to become unwell.

So although Miley was smiley on the outside,

she was not very smiley on the inside.

"If I fall over and scrape my paw, people

can see my paw is poorly.

But no one can see my poorly mind,"

she said to herself.

Because of this, she was scared that

no one would believe her.

After all, most folk thought she was

the happiest dog around.

Shhhhhh!

Therefore, she kept her
secret very, very secret.

But as the months passed, some people

continued to be cruel to Miley...

...and Miley still really missed

those she had lost.

Her smile was becoming much harder to wear.

She began to feel more and more...

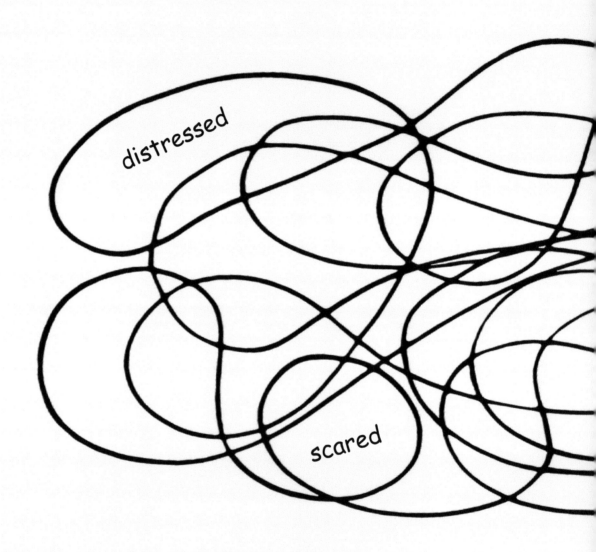

anxious

alone

Like a message in a bottle, she started to feel trapped.

Her tummy began to feel like a washing machine

that was spinning round really fast...

...and she felt like a huge, heavy weight

was pushing her to the ground.

She stopped singing to the sun.

She stopped dancing among the dew.

She no longer clapped the clouds when it rained.

She no longer burbled about her day to the moon.

Miley hid herself away.

Some days, she could not sleep and could not eat.

Other days, she would sleep too much

and eat until she felt sick.

However, Miley knew her life could be better.

She wanted to be smiley on the outside AND on the inside.

She also wanted the spiteful behaviour
to stop and the heartache to ease.

So Miley put on her imaginary superhero outfit

and did a VERY courageous thing...

She reached out and talked to her friend, Nova.

Miley spoke openly about her feelings,

finally revealing her poorly mind.

Nova listened and Nova helped.

Most importantly, Nova believed Miley's mind

was poorly even though she could not see it.

LISTENED

BELIEVED

SUPPORTED

ENCOURAGED

UNDERSTOOD

HELPED

ACCEPTED

She reassured Miley that lots of minds become poorly

because of nasty words and cruel behaviour by others.

She also explained this is completely normal.

Miley was not alone.

Many minds can also become poorly for no reason at all.

Sometimes, feeling sad or anxious can just happen!

Although it is scary to feel this way, the feelings do not last forever.

Miley was reassured that her mind would mend.

However, Nova mentioned that it might take time

and Miley would need to be patient and believe in herself.

The best thing you can do for a poorly mind is talk

to those you trust – perhaps a friend,

a parent, a carer, a teacher or a doctor.

They will help your mind get better.

Over time, Miley's mind started to heal.

It became easier for her to manage the grief...

...and Nova stopped the cruel words

and spiteful behaviour from hurting.

Once again, she sang to the sun

and danced among the dew.

When it rained, she clapped the clouds for helping

the flowers to bloom and burbled all about her day to the moon.

People say, "Gosh Miley, how smiley you are!"

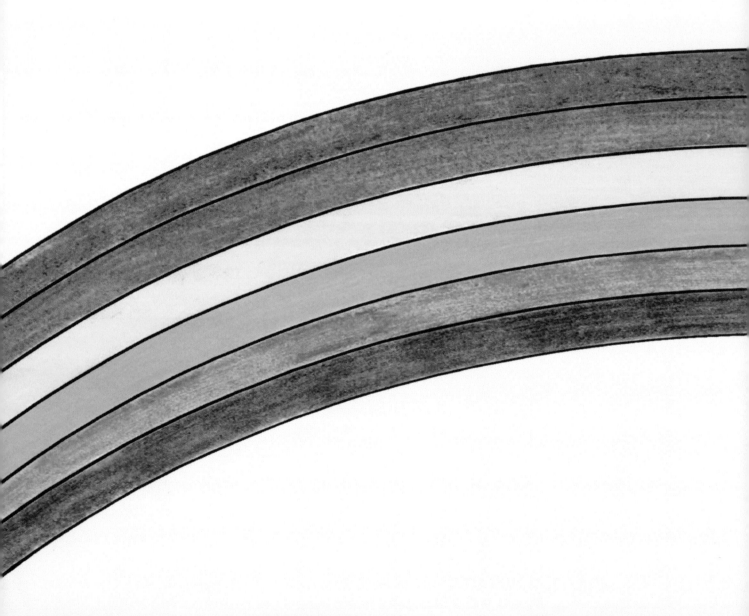

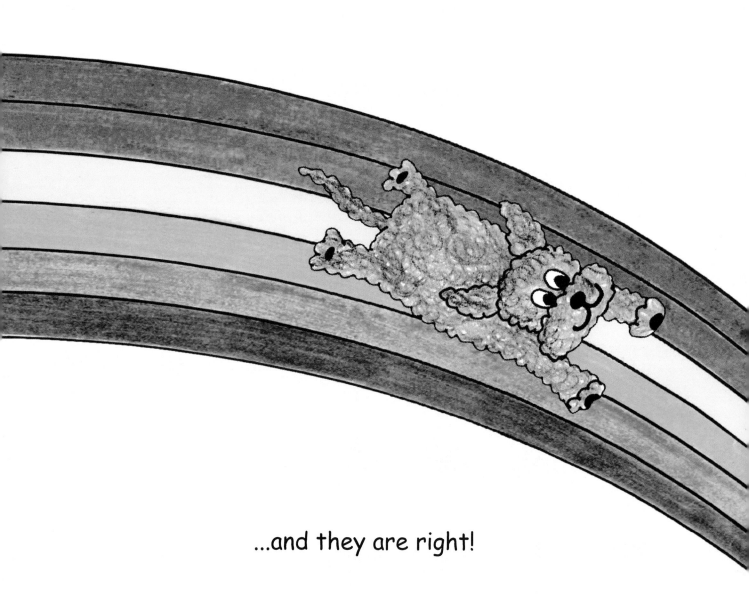

...and they are right!

Miley's Top Tip for Managing Anxiety

The 5-4-3-2-1 Coping Technique*

5 things you can see

4 things you can feel

3 things you can hear

2 things you can smell

1 thing you can taste

When you start to feel anxious, try this 5-4-3-2-1 coping technique.
First, look around and think of 5 things you can see.
Next, think of 4 things you can feel. Carry on through all the steps.
This will help ground you and ease any immediate anxious thoughts.

*https://www.urmc.rochester.edu/behavioral-health-partners/bhp-blog/april-2018/5-4-3-2-1-coping-technique-for-anxiety.aspx

About the Author

Katie lives in the West Midlands with her very special dog friend, Miley. Miley has helped Katie with her own anxiety and this was the main inspiration for this book.

Katie says,"I want this book to help children understand that it is okay to feel worried or scared and there are many people to help and support them."

Katie has worked with children, both in schools and in other childcare settings, since she was 16. She has seen a growing number of children experience anxiety and other mental health issues.

Symptoms of Anxiety in Children

🐾 Finding it hard to concentrate

🐾 Not sleeping, or waking in the night with bad dreams

🐾 Not eating properly

🐾 Quickly getting angry or irritable, and being out of control during outbursts

🐾 Constantly worrying or having negative thoughts

🐾 Feeling tense and fidgety, or using the toilet often

🐾 Always crying

🐾 Being clingy

🐾 Complaining of tummy aches and feeling unwell

Signs of Abuse in Children

🐾 Unexplained changes in behaviour or personality

🐾 Becoming withdrawn

🐾 Seeming anxious

🐾 Becoming uncharacteristically aggressive

🐾 Lacks social skills and has few or no friends

🐾 Poor bond or relationship with a parent

🐾 Knowledge of adult issues inappropriate for their age

🐾 Running away or going missing

🐾 Always choosing to wear clothes which cover their body

Signs of Bullying in Children

🐾 Your child comes home with torn, damaged, or missing pieces of clothing, books, or other belongings

🐾 Has unexplained cuts, bruises, and scratches

🐾 Has few, if any friends, with whom he or she spends time

🐾 Seems afraid of going to school, walking to and from school, riding the school bus, or taking part in organised activities with peers

🐾 Finds or makes up excuses as to why they can't go to school

🐾 Takes a long, out of the way, route when walking to or from school

If you require further information on the signs and symptons

of child anxiety, abuse and bullying you can

visit the NHS website, NSPCC website

and Stomp Out Bullying website.

All details of supportive agencies are detailed

on the following pages.

Useful Contact Details

General Mental Health

Mind

Phone: 0300 123 3393

Email: info@mind.org.uk

Text: 86463

Young Minds UK

Text (urgent help): YM to 85258

Phone (parents' helpline): 0808 802 5544

The Samaritans

Phone: 116 123

Email: jo@samaritans.org

Bullying

Bullying UK

Email: askus@familylives.org.uk

Phone: 0808 800 2222

Grief

Winston's Wish

Phone: 0808 802 0021

Eating Disorders

Beat

Phone (Helpline): 0808 801 0677

Phone (Studentline): 0808 801 0811

Phone (Youthline): 0808 801 0711

Abuse and/or Neglect

NSPCC

Phone (under 18s): 0800 1111

Phone (adult worried about a child): 0808 800 5000

Women's Aid

Email: helpline@womensaid.org.uk

Endorsements

"Miley's Mind is an important and useful book for all children and their carers. Katie Goodacre recognises the potentially damaging power of words and their ability to contribute to healing. In this book, she combines her awareness of lanuguage and child development to create a powerful tool for anyone interested in supporting children's mental health and wellbeing."

Dr Rachel Wicaksono - MA (Oxon), MA TESOL, EdD
Head of the School of Education, Language and Psychology, York St John University

"The themes and lessons covered in Miley's Mind have come at a critical time. We have seen social isolation increase and childhood recede. We need to start talking about mental health and talk about it earlier."

Dr Michael McArdle - MbChB, BSc (Hons)
Paediatric Accident and Emergency, Leeds Teaching Hospitals

"Katie Goodacre generates high levels of enthusiasm, participation and commitment to child progression and I've no doubt that Miley's Mind will be really helpful to children's mental health development."

Richard Holmes - CEO, The Kings Active Foundation

"A wonderful book that deals with the subject of children's mental health in a sensitive, but powerful way"

Tony Staneff - Director of Learning, Trinity Multi Academy Trust, Halifax

"Miley's Mind introduces what is often seen as a difficult and uncomfortable topic to young readers, and is carefully explored with calmness and sensitivity."

Matthew Marshall - Student Teacher, York St John University

Thank you - talk more and stay safe.

Katie and Miley

xxx

Printed in Poland
by Amazon Fulfillment
Poland Sp. z o.o., Wrocław

62925011R00033